MRS. McFINNY AND HER FRIENDS

Mrs. McFinny

AND HER FRIENDS

by

MARY T. SCHOONOVER

Illustrated by Helena Schoonover

New York · 1947

THE MACMILLAN COMPANY

To
Aunt Nell

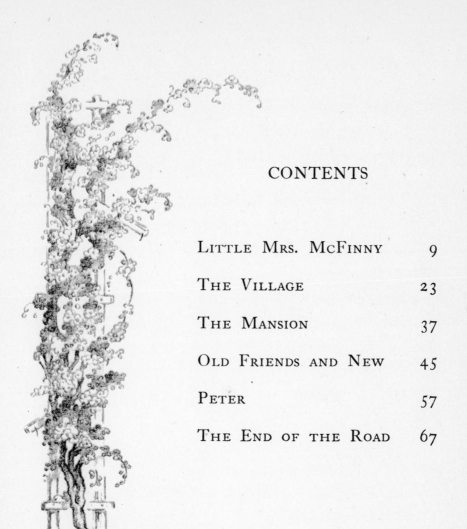

CONTENTS

1. Little Mrs. McFinny

Little Mrs. McFinny lived all alone with her dog and her cat in a little cottage at the foot of the hill and at the end of the road.

Few people ever went that way because it was the end of the road and most people like to keep on going. Once the little cottage had been very nice, with the paint all fresh and bright and the shingles all firm and strong. But, like Mrs. McFinny herself, the cottage was getting old. It was still very pretty in summer, with many flowers growing around it—a row of pink and white and yellow hollyhocks along one side and a row of pink and white and lavender phlox on the other; a mass of blue morning glories over the trellis at the kitchen door and a mass of white and pink roses growing over the trellis at the front door. At the back of the house, against the fence, there was a long row of berry-bushes from which Mrs. McFinny made those delicious jars of jam and jelly that stood on her pantry shelves.

Mrs. McFinny loved flowers, and people said she had a green thumb; but the truth is that all the flowers loved Mrs. McFinny and did their very best to cover up the places where the trellis was going to pieces, and all the other places, here and there, that needed mending. Oh, yes, it was still very pretty in the summer; but when cold weather came and the leaves and the flowers just couldn't keep on trying any longer and one by one fell sleepily to the ground, then Mrs. McFinny had to admit to herself that the cottage looked a bit the worse for wear.

Mrs. McFinny was a sweet little old lady. Her snow-white hair so soft and curly; her cheeks a bit wrinkled, perhaps, but as pink as roses; her eyes, blue and bright and merry. And then her smile! It was the most winning smile—it made one feel all warm inside, and even the crossest person would feel his crossness melt within him if she smiled at him.

Not that Mrs. McFinny was old in anything but years, and years don't count with a spirit as young as hers. True she wasn't as nimble and spry as she once had been and she couldn't help worrying a little when the roof began to leak around the chimney. But even that did not really discourage her. "The more hope and faith are needed, the more hope and faith one should have." So she placed a pan under the leak and hoped for the best!

Living as she did at the foot of the hill and at the end of the road, Mrs. McFinny would have been a bit lonely if it had not been for her dog and her cat.

Happy was the little dog's name and, besides being happy, he could be really useful. He was a good little watchdog and never failed, day or night, to let his mistress know if there was anyone around. Mrs. McFinny always felt perfectly safe when he was there; for, little as he was, he could growl and sound very fierce. Of course they both knew that his fierceness was all put on, for Happy wouldn't have hurt a fly and had never bitten anything except his own tail, once, when he was chasing it round and round. Happy also was a most wonderful little errand boy and had on that account won the respect and admiration of everybody in the little village half a mile away, on the other side of the hill.

But Happy wasn't the only one who could do things. Whiskers, the cat, could be useful too. When a house is as old as this one, somehow it is easy for mice to get in—and there wasn't so much to eat in the cottage that anything could be spared for the mice. All the mice around that neighborhood knew what a good mouser Whiskers was, how long and how patiently she would wait at that hole near the cellar stairs. No mouse had dared to come near it for a long time. And there were other things Whiskers could do, like cleaning up stray crumbs or any leftover odds and ends of food so as to keep them from spoiling.

Mrs. McFinny did very well with what she had, but she had so very little that it was a wonder she managed at all.

On the first day of the month there came to the little post office, in the village on the other side of the hill, a very large envelope addressed to Mrs. McFinny. Inside that very large envelope there was a very small check. Although it was a small check it brought a great deal of comfort to Mrs. McFinny, who never failed to be there at the post office to receive it. Mr. Dolittle, who kept the general store —the one and only store in the village—cashed the check for Mrs. McFinny and, to make it easier for her, turned it all into quarters, dimes, nickles, and pennies.

And so each month started off merrily enough, but toward the end of the month things were not quite so merry.

Indeed sometimes Happy felt that if he had worn a belt instead of a collar he would have had to take a notch in it. Whiskers got on a little better, because she was smaller and, besides, she often went fishing in the brook—that lovely brook that circled the foot of the hill.

In spite of their ups and downs, all in all they lived very happily together—Mrs. McFinny, Happy, and Whiskers. Even being poor didn't seem to bother them very much. Anyway they never mentioned the fact but always made the best of things.

Mrs. McFinny had always been a wonderful house-keeper—the kind that keeps the corners clean, as well as the places that show, and that makes the kettles shine—and her cooking was even better than her housekeeping. When

Mr. McFinny was living, she had made him the most delicious pies and cakes and muffins and bread—real homemade bread, so crisp and brown on the outside, so white and springy on the inside.

And the cooky jar had always been full then. Mrs. McFinny still baked her own bread and still tried to keep some cookies in her jar. She liked to have something to

16

offer the farmer's boy who so kindly brought her a big pail of milk every once in a while, and sometimes even some cream for her to make into nice yellow butter. It was good of the farmer to send the milk, for it meant a great deal to Mrs. McFinny as well as to Whiskers and Happy. So, what with her housekeeping and her flowers and her berries and the few vegetables she tried to raise, Mrs. McFinny was as busy as the day was long.

In the evening when her supper was over and her work was all done and Happy and Whiskers had gone for a final frolic, Mrs. McFinny would light her oil lamp and sit down to read from her Bible for a while. When she became sleepy she would rise, put her Bible away, shake down the fire and, if the dog and cat had come in, she would lock the doors and they would all go to bed.

Happy was always sure to be in—he didn't like to be out at night—but Whiskers wasn't always there when she should have been, and had to be called and called. "Why do cats want to be out when they ought to be in?" asked Happy of himself. Then he would step outside the door and bark loud and long. That never failed to bring Whiskers running. It wasn't that she minded Happy better than Mrs. McFinny, but Mrs. McFinny's voice was small and gentle, like Mrs. McFinny herself, and Whiskers had been a long way off.

Then, at last, Mrs. McFinny could go to bed in her big four-poster. It was such a big four-poster and Mrs. McFinny was so little that, when she had pulled up the covers and tucked the sheet under her chin, with her snow-white hair and the snow-white pillow, if it hadn't been that her cheeks

were so pink and her eyes so blue, one would hardly have known she was there!

Happy and Whiskers always waited till Mrs. McFinny had put out her light before they settled down. Then Whiskers, the mouser, lay down in her basket not far from the hole by the cellar stairs, just in case a mouse should make so bold as to try his luck, and Happy, the faithful watchdog, lay on the rug by the door. Then sleep fell like a blessing on the little house at the end of the road.

2. The Village

On the other side of the hill, and at the beginning of the road that led to Mrs. McFinny's little house, was the village.

The principal buildings in the village were the church, the schoolhouse, and the general store.

The small post office to which Mrs. McFinny went once a month to get her check was not in a building of its own but was housed in the general-store building, of which Mr. Dolittle was the owner.

This building was large, square, and flat, and it would
have been nothing at all to look at but that it had a false
front which made it look much larger than it was. From
across the street the building looked quite handsome; but
if one looked at it from the side, one could see that the upper
half was just make-believe.

As one went in at the front door, the post-office part was
partitioned off to the right and in the front partition was a
little window where Mrs. Dolittle, the postmistress, sat and
handed out the mail.

She was a sharp little woman and from that little window she kept a sharp eye on everyone and on everything

that went on in the store. Like the building she, too, had a false front—a set of curls that she pinned on every morning, to cover up the bald spot on the top of her head. Nobody was supposed to know that those curls did not grow on her head and, of course, no one ever mentioned them.

In the middle of the store there was a big iron stove around which all the notable people of the village—such as the barber, the blacksmith, and the tax collector—gathered every evening all year to settle the affairs of the world.

The rest of the store was full of things to sell—things to eat and to wear, and things for the farm.

It was a really fine general store, and people came to it from far and near because it was such a good store; but the best thing about it was Mr. Dolittle himself. He was big and broad and warmhearted and there was no false front about him. The corner of the store that Mr. Dolittle liked best was where the candy and cooky counter stood. It was here that Mrs. McFinny brought her gingerbread cookies when her funds were getting low, toward the end of the month.

Mr. Dolittle had to juggle his figures a bit when Mrs. Dolittle looked over his accounts; for he not only paid Mrs. McFinny very well for her cookies but he also ate most of them himself, on the sly. They were such very good cookies! But, of course, if one eats one's cookies, one cannot possibly sell them too. Mr. Dolittle was very glad, sometimes, that the post-office part of the store was partitioned off and that the window was not on the side where the candy and cooky case stood.

While the store was very important to the people of the village, the most important building was the church—a lovely old colonial church with great pillars in front and a high steeple that pointed up as if to say, "Look up, for God is there."

The people of that section thought the world of their church and kept it in good repair. The sexton also took great pride in it, almost as though it belonged to him.

The thing the sexton liked to do best was to ring the bell—that lovely old bell 'way up in the steeple that rang out so sweetly and clearly that it could be heard even on the other side of the hill.

29

The sound seemed to have a queer effect on Happy; for when he heard it, he would lift up his head and howl. Mrs. McFinny wondered why Happy howled. She thought perhaps he was trying to sing and he looked so very funny, with his head lifted up and his eyes rolling, that Whiskers and she could not help laughing at him.

Mrs. McFinny went to church as often as she could when the weather was good. Happy had offered to go with her many a time, but his mistress would not let him. He would go with her to the top of the hill, and then Mrs. McFinny would tell him to be a good little dog and run back home to take care of things and to keep Whiskers out of mischief till she came back.

30

Happy wondered why he was welcome anywhere except in church, and finally made up his mind to find out. When the next Sunday came around he pretended to be asleep and paid no attention to Mrs. McFinny as she started out, but she had no sooner gone over the crest of the hill than Happy jumped up and ran after her.

It was a beautiful spring morning and the sexton had left the doors open to let in the lovely spring air, so Happy had no trouble getting in. He stood at the door for a minute and looked around for Mrs. McFinny, but the seats were full and he could not see her at all.

Way up front on a platform stood a man in a long black robe, and behind and above him was a row of people also in black.

Happy did not like the look of it; but since he had come, he felt he had better see what it was all about. So he trotted up the middle aisle and sat down right in front of the minister. Putting his head to one side, he cocked his ears the better to see and hear what was going on. But he had no sooner settled there than someone had him by the collar

32

—and the first thing he knew Happy was out on the road and the doors were being closed firmly behind him!

Happy felt very much hurt and ashamed and he looked quickly around to make sure that no other dog had seen him being put out of the church; but luck was with him, for the street was empty.

So Happy trotted up the hill and then down again on the other side, and when Mrs. McFinny came home from church she found him lying just exactly where she had left him. In fact, he looked so sleepy and innocent that she almost thought she must have fallen asleep in church and dreamed it all.

33

If the grownups liked to go to church, the place the children liked to go to was the school. The schoolhouse was set in a nice playground, with swings and seesaws and a croquet field, and the classroom was fitted with the finest of everything.

But the nicest thing about the school was the teacher herself. Her name was Miss Rose, and not only was she the best teacher anywhere but she had such a way with her that everyone wanted to do what she said and everyone tried hard to please her.

34

Every morning when it was time for lessons to begin she would come and stand at the schoolhouse door and swing a big hand bell back and forth. She was so little and the bell was so big that it almost seemed as though the bell was swinging her, instead of her swinging the bell.

The last period of the day was the best of all. When lessons were done and everything made tidy, then Miss Rose would tell the children a story, stories of people and of animals who had done brave deeds—kind and gentle deeds that made the world a better place to live in. How the children loved the story hour and the sweet teacher who told the stories so well!

3. The Mansion

On the top of the hill and halfway between the village and Mrs. McFinny's little house, there was a large and handsome iron gate set in a stone wall that ran around a beautiful park.

A broad driveway went up a gentle slope from the gate to a large ivy-covered stone mansion. The place was very beautiful, but it had been deserted for years and, except for the occasional footsteps of the caretaker, the only sounds to be heard were the singing of birds and the chattering of squirrels.

But recently Mr. Jonathan Stone, a very rich man from the great city, had bought the mansion and had come to live there with his little boy. Mr. Stone was a tall, handsome, but rather hard-looking man. He had made lots of money but seemed always to want to make more, and the wise men who gathered around Mr. Dolittle's stove said that money was all that Mr. Stone cared for.

If they had only known, Mr. Stone's hard look was very much like Mrs. Dolittle's false front—it was there to cover up something. Mr. Stone would have been ashamed to let anyone see how kind a heart was hidden by that false front.

Mr. Stone's little boy was a fine little boy and his name was Peter. At first he was so glad to be in the country, instead of the big city, that he was pleased with everything and could be seen running around the beautiful park chasing the squirrels, talking to the birds, and having a wonderful time. But little by little he began to find it rather lonely.

Peter would have liked to go to school, to the pretty schoolhouse of which he had caught a glimpse as he drove through the village the day he arrived. But a common village school was no place for the son of a man who had made so much money. So a tutor from a near-by town was engaged to come every day to teach Peter. At nine every morning the lessons began and, although Peter was a good boy and always learned his lessons and did his homework, it was lonely work. Peter's thoughts often wandered to the happy children playing around the little schoolhouse in the village. He often thought of asking his father, of whom he was a bit afraid, if some of those children might not be invited to come and play with him, but he did not dare.

At noon the lessons ended and the tutor went away and soon Peter was called to have luncheon in the big, stiff dining room, where the chairs were so high that poor Peter's feet could not reach the floor and just dangled in the air.

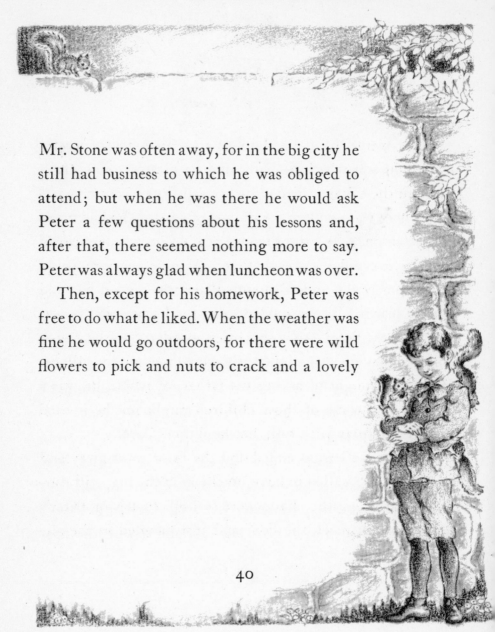

Mr. Stone was often away, for in the big city he still had business to which he was obliged to attend; but when he was there he would ask Peter a few questions about his lessons and, after that, there seemed nothing more to say. Peter was always glad when luncheon was over.

Then, except for his homework, Peter was free to do what he liked. When the weather was fine he would go outdoors, for there were wild flowers to pick and nuts to crack and a lovely

stream that raced down the hill toward Mrs. McFinny's.
But sooner or later Peter always came up against that high
stone wall that divided Mr. Stone's land from everyone
else's, and except for the squirrels, which grew quite tame
and even ate out of his pocket, Peter was always alone.

One day Peter made a wonderful discovery. Not far from
the big gate, and completely hidden by some thick lilac
bushes, he discovered a door in the wall. It was a small door
and its bolt and hinges were covered with rust, but to Peter's
joy he was able to push back the bolt and to pull the door

open a little. He closed it right away, for he was pretty sure that he was not supposed to know about it; but he was glad he did, just the same, even though he did not mean to use it.

And so Peter fell into the habit of standing by the gate—that big gate that was always locked. But, although it was locked, Peter could at least see through it—which was more than he could do with the wall. Peter hoped very hard that, sometime, someone or something nice would go by. But nothing ever did.

He did not know that the road that went by the gate led only to Mrs. McFinny's and that Mrs. McFinny did not leave her house very often. But still Peter waited by the gate . . . and one day his patience was rewarded.

4. *Old Friends and New*

The lovely stream that raced down the hill back of Mr. Stone's mansion was the very same stream in which Whiskers went fishing, only it had become a quiet, lazy stream by the time it reached the foot of the hill by Mrs. McFinny's little house. It murmured softly as it slid over the little stones and it gurgled merrily as it slid around the larger stones that lay in its bed. Here and there it made a quiet little pool in which little fishes played about in the sunshine, and in which the trees and flowers on the bank admired their own reflections.

Whiskers loved the stream, especially when the sun was shining. In the middle of it there was a stone, flat and wide, which she could reach quite easily and where she loved to lie and sun herself. As she lay there so quietly, she kept a sharp lookout in the hope that some rash little fish might come within her reach.

But Whiskers's fishing was mostly make-believe—something to boast about to Happy, who could do so many things that Whiskers could not. Sometimes when Happy was coming back from his errands at the store, Whiskers would walk slowly from the direction of the stream making a great show of licking her chops. Then she would stop and wash her face as all nice pussies do when they have just had a good meal.

Of course it was mostly make-believe. Whiskers hated to wet her paws—the very look of water made her lift her paw and shake it as if she were shaking the water off.

However, once in a while she did catch something. And once when Mrs. McFinny was looking a bit worried—it was getting near the time for the tax collector to come around—Whiskers had caught a nice fat fish and, instead of feasting on it there and then, had brought it to where Mrs. McFinny was working in the garden and laid it down at her feet.

Then Whiskers looked up and positively grinned!

The check which Mrs. McFinny received on the first of the month was not the only mail that came for her to the little post office in the village on the other side of the hill. Oh, no! Hardly a day passed but a letter or a card came out of the mailbag that Mrs. Dolittle handled so well. Mrs. McFinny was so sweet that anyone who' had met her, even once, became her friend. And the only way to keep friendship alive when people are separated is by writing letters.

Mrs. McFinny loved to read her mail and, just as long as she was able, every afternoon when her work was done she took that long walk to the post office. Of course Happy went with her and often carried a small package for her in his mouth. Whiskers had tried to go too, but she could not keep up without running and she soon gave it up and went fishing instead.

But the time came when Mrs. McFinny was not strong enough to take that long walk very often, and then Mr. Dolittle had a wonderful idea. Feeling sure that Happy was such a smart little dog that he could do Mrs. McFinny's errands by himself if given a chance, Mr. Dolittle made a little saddle, which fitted Happy comfortably, and then fastened a small market basket very securely to the saddle.

48

How funny Happy looked with it on! The basket reached from the back of his collar almost to his tail! What was to go into the basket would not weigh very much. Sometimes Mrs. McFinny needed a few groceries, but all her wants were so very small.

When the day of the great experiment came, Mrs. Mc-Finny wrote a little note, put it into a paper bag along with a little money, and placed it in the basket. After she had fastened the basket to Happy's saddle she talked to him very gently and told him that she was too tired to go to the store that day and so she was asking him to go alone.

49

Happy listened very quietly; then he barked a couple of times as if to say, "I understand, and you can depend on me." And very proud and happy he looked as he started out!

When he reached the store he scratched at the door a little, and Mr. Dolittle, who had been on the lookout for him, opened the door and let him in. Then Mr. Dolittle read the note and counted the pennies and filled the order. He always saved a bone for Happy and a few scraps of meat for Whiskers, and these went into the basket too. Then Happy, as he had been in the habit of doing, trotted over to the post-office window and barked.

Even the sharp Mrs. Dolittle softened at the thought of Mrs. McFinny and, after she had come out at the side door and tucked in the mail, she covered the basket with yesterday's newspaper so that Mrs. McFinny might keep up with the times. Then Mr. Dolittle gave Happy a pat on the head, calling him a smart little dog, opened the door and said, "Now, Happy, go home like a good little dog"—and away Happy went. But first he took a drink at the fountain, for the village had a fine fountain with a drinking place for horses and one for dogs.

50

When Happy reached home safely that day Mrs. Mc-Finny made a great fuss over him and told him that he was the most wonderful little helper anyone could have. And from that day on, if Mrs. McFinny was feeling tired or had too much to do, Happy, like the faithful little dog he was, went on that long walk to the post office alone.

One day, when he had started a little later than usual on his errands, just as he reached the top of the hill Happy saw a little boy standing inside the big iron gate looking out at the road. When the boy saw Happy and his basket, he laughed and whistled softly for the dog to come nearer to the gate.

51

Happy stopped for a minute and lifted one paw as if to shake hands, for he was a very polite little dog. But then he remembered the money in the basket and thought perhaps he had better go on. Still, Happy said to himself, the boy did not smell like a tramp. Happy was very careful about tramps and always hid behind a bush or something if he saw someone coming. So he decided not to stop and went on to the village, but when he came back the little boy was still standing there. The same thing happened the next day—only this time when Happy was returning from the store he

found the little boy standing on the outside of the gate, for Peter had slipped out through the little door in the garden wall.

So there Peter was, and so they went home together to Mrs. McFinny's. Peter didn't feel that he was doing very wrong, because no one paid much attention to him after lessons were over—especially when Mr. Stone was away, as he was just then. Mrs. McFinny was in the garden, with Whiskers, covering up the rosebushes before the coming of winter.

As soon as she saw the little boy she put down her tools and, stooping, gave him a big loving hug, and Peter, who never in his life had been hugged before, began to feel all warm inside and thought he had never seen anything as sweet as this little old lady.

It didn't take Mrs. McFinny and Peter very long to become fast friends and to find how many things they had in common, like loving flowers and birds and sunshine and, perhaps, like both being a bit lonely too.

So they all went inside to put away the things from Happy's basket. And then Mrs. McFinny brought out the cooky jar!

5. Peter

A very important piece of business kept Mr. Stone in the city for almost two weeks and those were the happiest weeks Peter had ever known. No one at the big house even suspected that every afternoon Peter slipped out of the little door in the wall and together with Happy, his new-found friend, ran down the hill to Mrs. McFinny's.

These were very happy days also for Mrs. McFinny, who, although she loved her dog and her cat as much as any dog and cat had ever been loved before, still had a lot of love left over for anyone who needed it, and Peter seemed to need it very much.

During those two weeks Peter found out a lot of things about Mrs. McFinny and her house, and Mrs. McFinny found out a lot of things about Peter—such as how much he wanted to go to that little red schoolhouse in the village, instead of having lessons with a tutor, and how he longed to have some boys and girls to play with. Another thing Mrs. McFinny found out was that Peter would be eight years old on Friday. Mrs. McFinny seemed to think that was wonderful and she told Peter she would have a little party for him and they would celebrate together.

Peter always took care not to stay too long at Mrs. McFinny's for fear someone would miss him. When he went home on the day before his birthday he learned from the housekeeper that his father was expected home next morning, but when morning came his father did not come.

Peter was very much excited about the party and could hardly wait for his lessons to be over. Then followed luncheon in the dining room, with that big footman standing so stiffly back of his chair. It always made Peter nervous to have him stand there. But at last that was over also, and at two o'clock Peter, bundled up in a coat and cap and mittens, went out into the park.

It was cold and an inch or two of soft sparkling

58

snow had fallen in the night and the world was like fairyland. Peter went to the gate and waited; but he hadn't long to wait, for Happy was always on time. Peter was sure that Happy knew it was all a secret, because Happy never barked at all but only winked at him as he went by. Then Peter went round to the little door back of the lilac bushes and slipped out. It seemed like a long time to Peter, waiting there; but at last Happy came back from the store and off they went together down the hill.

What Peter had not thought of was that each step he took in that crisp carpet of snow could be clearly seen and that anyone looking for him could easily follow him.

Mrs. McFinny met Peter at the door with a cheerful "Happy Birthday, Peter," and she kissed him gently on the cheek. Then she helped him off with his things and, after he had petted Whiskers a few minutes, they all went

59

into the little dining room. There the table was set with Mrs. McFinny's best tablecloth and her lovely old china cups, as white and pink and frail as herself.

In the middle of the table was a fine birthday cake with white frosting and little pink roses and in the middle the words "Happy Birthday." Around the edge were eight little candles that Mrs. McFinny had made herself, for there seemed no end to the things that Mrs. McFinny could do.

Then Mrs. McFinny put the teakettle on and soon Peter was sitting down to a wonderful tea, with Mrs. McFinny's good bread, still warm from the oven, and homemade butter and jam. But first Whiskers, who loved a saucerful of tea with lots of cream and a sprinkle of sugar, and Happy, who liked a slice of bread with butter and jam, had to be served. They had theirs on the hearthstone so as not to soil the worn, but spotless, carpet.

60

Mrs. McFinny and Peter had no sooner sat down at the table than there came a great knocking at the door. And who should walk in but Mr. Stone, who had made a great effort to get back in time for Peter's birthday and had been badly frightened when Peter could not be found! He and the servants had searched everywhere and at last Mr. Stone had spotted the telltale footprints in the snow that led to the little door in the wall and then down the hill to the little house at the end of the road.

You can just imagine what a state he was in! "A fine scare you gave me, young man," he said, looking fiercely at Peter. "How was I to know where you had gone, you little scamp?"

Peter always felt very small when his father spoke to him. Now he felt no larger than one of the horse chestnuts that rolled about in the park. Swallowing hard, in a weak little voice he said, "I never thought anyone would miss me, Father." But here Mrs. McFinny spoke up and asked Mr. Stone if he would not join them at the table, because they were having a little birthday party. And to everyone's astonishment, especially to his own, Mr. Stone did sit down and soon was eating bread and butter and jam as if he had seen no food for a week!

It was not long before Mr. Stone began to grow all warm inside and a nice comfortable feeling spread all through him such as he had not felt for years. All sorts of old memories swept over him and he put down his cup and for a moment forgot where he was.

But he was soon called back to earth by the excited laughter of Peter, who was cutting his birthday cake and

trying not to spill it. First he put a small piece on a plate and placed it in front of Mrs. McFinny, and then he put a large piece on a plate and as he placed it in front of his father he said timidly, "Father, did you ever see such a lovely cake?"

64

And as Peter looked at his father he saw that something had happened. That stern mask that Mr. Stone had worn so long had disappeared. Perhaps it was the sight of Mrs. McFinny's sweet face, perhaps it was the sight of his little boy's happiness, but the false front was not there any more.

Peter had never before seen that gentle look and all his fear of his father slipped away.

Pretty soon Peter was telling his father all about his new friends: of Happy and his market basket, of Whiskers and her fishing, of the leak in the roof near the chimney, and of the hole that Whiskers had to watch to keep the mice from coming in—and even of how it was nearly time for the tax collector to come around, and lots of other things that Mrs. McFinny would not have told for the world!

Mr. Stone sat listening quietly to all that Peter had to say and, though he pretended not to hear when Peter mentioned things like the tax collector, he put it all away in a little corner of his mind to think over later. But, knowing how uncomfortable Mrs. McFinny must be, when Peter finally had to stop for breath, Mr. Stone broke in, "It's my turn, young man. I suppose you thought I had forgotten all about your birthday. Well, I hadn't. I was going to give you this after dinner, but I think Mrs. McFinny would like me to give it to you now."

And then he pulled a little box out of his pocket and pushed it over toward Peter.

In that box was a sturdy little wrist watch in a leather guard and strap, and when Peter had taken it out, to see it better, he saw on the back of the watch the words "To Peter from Daddy."

Peter gave a little gasp and, looking up, said softly, "Oh, Daddy!"

When Mrs. McFinny's eyes met Mr. Stone's, each saw that the other's were bright with tears.

6. *The End of the Road*

Next morning when Peter was having his stuffy lessons with his tutor, Mr. Stone put on his coat and hat and quietly, without anyone seeing him, went out of the house, down the driveway and out of the little door in the wall, then on down the hill to the little house at the end of the road.

When Mrs. McFinny had let him in, Mr. Stone told her in a rather gruff voice that he had come on business and strictly on business. He told her that he wanted to buy her place, that to him it was valuable because he was about to buy some land beyond hers, and that unless she would sell to him his property would be divided. Besides, he was interested in the stream because of its good fishing.

He offered Mrs. McFinny a sum which to her seemed very large and told her that, of course, he would expect her to stay and take care of the place for him as long as she lived. And then he added, more gently, that he hoped she would advise him about Peter once in a while and help to bring him up.

Mrs. McFinny wasn't a bit fooled by Mr. Stone's businesslike tone. She had seen through him from the first and had seen how dreadfully frightened he had been when Peter couldn't be found. So she laughed a little and then she cried a little and then she put her hands on his arm and said, very simply, that she thanked him from the bottom of her heart, and then she added that he would never know what a relief it would be to stop pretending that she wasn't worried.

By and by, when her tears were all dried, she said, "There is something I would like to say about Peter. What the boy needs most is to be with boys and girls his own age. Now think, Mr. Stone, how would you have liked a tutor when you were eight? Miss Rose, the village teacher, would be like a mother to him. As for me, I can only be his Granny."

"Probably you are right," said Mr. Stone, and he promised to think it over.

"Christmas is coming and the goose is getting fat," shouted Peter as he rushed into Mrs. McFinny's kitchen a couple of days before Christmas. He was carrying a great wreath of holly that almost covered him up, and just behind him came the big stiff footman—only he wasn't stiff any more because he was bent almost double under the weight of a huge basket, which he set down on the kitchen table with a sigh of relief.

"Merry Christmas," said Peter. And "Merry Christmas," said the footman as he turned to go, and "Merry Christmas to you," said Mrs. McFinny as she let him out. Then, turning to look at the basket on the table, she said,

"Oh, my! Oh, my! What have we here?" And Peter answered, "A big fat goose with all the trimmings: cranberries and pickles, olives and celery, mincemeat and nuts; oranges, grapes, and sugar plums; and a big round plum pudding! Daddy sent it all, with his best wishes to the dearest little lady in the world! And he did not forget Happy and Whiskers, for there is a bone for Happy and a can of salmon for Whiskers."

At that, Whiskers, who had been watching every move from the shelf above the table, licked her chops; and Happy, from the chair on which he had climbed, barked loud and long—which was their way of saying, "Thank you, Peter."

"And will Peter and his Daddy come and have Christmas dinner with me?" asked Mrs. McFinny as she wiped away a tear with the corner of her apron.

"If you promise not to tell," answered Peter, "I'll tell you a secret. That is what Daddy and I hoped you would say, but he told me to tell you that you must promise not to work too hard."

When Mrs. McFinny had looked her fill at all the lovely things in the basket, Peter untied the bunch of mistletoe that was fastened to its handle and said, "Let's go and tie

this up in the middle of the curtain rod in the sitting-room doorway."

And so Peter took the kitchen ladder-stool and, followed by Mrs. McFinny with the mistletoe and Happy with the ribbon, went into the sitting room and hung up the mistletoe with the help of Whiskers, who climbed up beside him.

When this was done, Peter stepped partway down till his face was on a level with Mrs. McFinny's and, putting his arms around her, he said, "Do you know what? Daddy went to see Miss Rose, and I am to begin going to school the first of the year. Oh, Granny," he said, giving her a big long hug, "this is the most wonderful Christmas I have ever known!"

Christmas day broke clear and sunny and Mrs. McFinny was up bright and early, for there was much to do in preparation for the grand dinner she had planned for her guests from the mansion at the top of the hill.

But first of all came breakfast for herself and her two pets. Mrs. McFinny put on the coffeepot and, while she was waiting for it to boil, took out the wonderful bone Peter had brought, and which she had cooked the day before. "Never was so much meat called a bone before," thought Mrs. McFinny as she filled Whiskers's dish with little pieces. The rest was for Happy.

Happy and Whiskers watched her every move with great interest, but waited patiently side by side till their breakfasts were set before them.

Then "Merry Christmas," said Mrs. McFinny. "Merry

74

Christmas," said Happy with two loud barks. "Merry Christmas," purred Whiskers softly, looking up into the sweet face she loved so well.

Happy picked up his bone and waited at the door till Mrs. McFinny let him out; for, no matter how much meat there might be on it, a bone was a bone and the place to eat it was outdoors, where he could growl over it to his heart's content—guarding it against his imaginary enemies. But Whiskers liked her meals best by the warm kitchen stove, and there her soft purr mingled happily with the bubble of the coffeepot.

Mrs. McFinny did not sit long over her breakfast, for there was much to do if the grand dinner she had planned was to be ready in time. She had always loved to cook and so she was happier preparing that Christmas dinner than she had been for years.

When everything was cooked and ready to serve, Mrs. McFinny took off her apron and went into her bedroom to put on her best print dress and smooth her hair so as to be ready to greet her guests. And she was just in time, for no sooner was it done than there came a great rattling at the door.

As she hastened to open it, in ran Peter fairly bursting with excitement and shouting "Merry Christmas" at the top of his lungs. His father, who came in after him, was trying to look businesslike and calm as he added his greeting to Peter's, but in reality he was almost as excited as Peter and felt just like a boy on a holiday.

Happy, who had been out making sure that his bone was safely buried, followed them in and barked his head off in welcome—so much so that Whiskers became alarmed and withdrew behind the stove. But not for long, for as soon as the noise had died down a little and Mrs. McFinny, with wonderful skill, was serving the food and placing it, piping hot, on the table, the scent proved too much for Whiskers and she came out to join in the fun.

And what fun it was, and what a dinner it turned out to be! The goose done to a turn; the gravy so rich and brown; the stuffing, biscuits, vegetables, jelly—everything just perfect! When at last Mr. Stone, who insisted on helping, carried in the flaming plum pudding and set it on the table, Peter just squealed for joy.

Peter had the time of his life that day, and perhaps what

he enjoyed most was the fact that there was no big silent footman standing stiffly behind his chair.

That evening, when the guests were gone, the dishes washed, the leftover food carefully stored away, and the last shining kettle hung up on its hook, Mrs. McFinny took off her apron and sat down happily in her great big armchair.

The great log fire that Mr. Stone had built in the fireplace had died down to a pile of glowing embers. Happy and Whiskers were lying contentedly, one on each side of the warm hearth, lazily watching their mistress through half-closed eyes. All was quiet except for Whiskers's purring and the occasional soft thump of Happy's short tail on the floor.

Mrs. McFinny was much too tired to read, but she took up her Bible and held it lovingly in her hands. Hers had been a happy day, happy in the happiness of her friends—her old friends, Happy and Whiskers, and her new friends, Peter and his father. And now the day was over and she could look back on it with pleasure and, because her new friends had been so good to her, she could also look forward with pleasure to the days to come.

Mrs. McFinny thought of Peter—dear Peter who had

brought something new and precious into her life. Her eyes wandered around the familiar room and rested on her faithful pets upon the hearthstone. How peaceful, friendly, and secure it seemed!

Out of the fullness of her grateful heart there rose a prayer of thanksgiving to the Good Lord who had sent so much happiness to the little house at the end of the road.